In every Mr Men and Little Miss book like this one, <u>and now</u> in the Mr Men sticker and activity books, you will find a special token. Collect six tokens and we will send you a gift of your choice

Choose either a <u>Mr Men</u> or <u>Little Miss</u> poster, **or** a Mr Men or Little Miss **double sided** full colour bedroom door hanger.

Return this page **with six tokens per gift required** to:

Marketing Dept., MM / LM, World International Ltd.,
PO Box 7, Manchester, M19 2HD

Your name:_____ Age: _____

Address: _____

_____

_____Postcode: _____

Parent / Guardian Name (Please Print)_____

|← 100 mm →|

ENTRANCE FEE 3 SAUSAGES

250 mm

MR. GREEDY

Please tape a 20p coin to your request to cover part post and package cost

I enclose <u>six</u> tokens per gift, and 20p please send me:-

<u>Posters:-</u>	Mr Men Poster		Little Miss Poster	☐
<u>Door Hangers</u> -	Mr Nosey / Muddle		Mr Greedy / Lazy	☐
	Mr Tickle / Grumpy		Mr Slow / Busy	☐
20p	Mr Messy / Quiet		Mr Perfect / Forgetful	☐
	L Miss Fun / Late		L Miss Helpful / Tidy	☐
	L Miss Busy / Brainy	☐	L Miss Star / Fun	☐

Stick 20p here please

Please Tick Appropriate Box

Collect six of these tokens
You will find one inside every
Mr Men and Little Miss book
which has this special offer.

1 TOKEN

We may occasionally wish to advise you of other Mr Men gifts.
If you would rather we didn't please tick this box   ☐

Offer open to residents of UK, Channel Isles and Ireland only

little Miss Greedy

by Roger Hargreaves

WORLD INTERNATIONAL

Little Miss Greedy certainly was.

What?

Greedy!

I'll say.
As greedy as a giant!
And giants are really very greedy indeed.

Little Miss Greedy lived in Cherrycake Cottage.

One lovely summer morning, a Monday,
Little Miss Greedy awoke earlier than usual.

She felt rather hungry, and so she went
into her kitchen and cooked herself
some breakfast.

Some breakfast indeed!

Sausages!

Now if you had sausages for breakfast,
or if I had sausages for breakfast,
how many sausages would we have?

One?
Perhaps two?
Maybe three?

Guess how many sausages Little Miss Greedy
had for breakfast.

Sixty-six!

Go on, count them!

Sixty-six succulent, sizzling sausages.

Which is difficult to say.

And even more difficult to eat.

Unless you're Little Miss Greedy!

Little Miss Greedy cut the last sausage on her plate in two, and popped one half into her mouth.

"Mmm!" she sighed, contentedly.
"That was nice," she thought to herself.
"Now what else shall I have?"

Guess what?

Toast!

Now if you had toast for breakfast,
or if I had toast for breakfast,
how many slices would we have?

Perhaps two?
Maybe three?

Guess how many slices of toast
Little Miss Greedy had for breakfast.

Twenty-three!
Twenty-three thick, tasty slices of tempting toast!
And marmalade.

Just as Little Miss Greedy was licking
the last crumb of the twenty-third slice
of toast from her lips, there was a knock
at the door of Cherrycake Cottage.

It was the postman.

"Letter for you, Little Miss Greedy," he said,
cheerfully.

"Oh good," smiled Little Miss Greedy,
for she liked it when someone sent her a letter.

"Would you like a cup of tea while you're here?"
she asked. "I'm going to have one."

One indeed!

Just look at the size of Little Miss Greedy's teapot!

The postman had one cup of tea and a chat, thanked Little Miss Greedy, and left.

Little Miss Greedy poured herself another cup (another after the eleven other cups she'd already had) and opened her letter.

It was from her cousin, Mr Greedy.

'Dear Little Miss Greedy,' he had written.
(He always wrote to his cousin this way.)

'Next Wednesday is my birthday.
Please come to tea at 4 o'clock.'

Little Miss Greedy was delighted.

She hadn't seen her cousin for
quite some time.

Wednesday was a lovely day.

After a little light lunch (I'll tell you what later),
Little Miss Greedy set off in her car to drive
to Mr Greedy's house.

But before she set off, she put something on
the back seat of her car.

Something large.

Mr Greedy's birthday present.

At 4 o'clock precisely, Little Miss Greedy pulled up in front of Mr Greedy's roly-poly sort of a house.

Mr Greedy was there to meet her.

"Hello, Little Miss Greedy," he smiled.
"How lovely to see you after all this time!"

"Happy birthday," laughed Little Miss Greedy, and she gave Mr Greedy a big kiss.

Mr Greedy blushed.

"Do come in," he said. "Tea's all ready!"

Little Miss Greedy was following Mr Greedy into
his house when she remembered something.
You know what it was, don't you?
That's right.
Mr Greedy's birthday present!

"Wait a minute," she said. "Can you help me to
lift something out of the back of my car, please?"
She smiled.
"It's rather heavy," she added.
"Certainly," agreed Mr Greedy.

There, on the back seat of Little Miss Greedy's car, was the biggest birthday cake you've ever seen in all your life.

A huge, enormous, gigantic, colossal currant cake, with thick pink icing on top and strawberry jam in the middle.

"I only put one candle on it," explained Little Miss Greedy as they carried it to the house, "because I've forgotten how old you are!"

"Oh, you shouldn't have," laughed Mr Greedy. He licked his lips. "But I'm glad you did!"

"I baked it today," said Little Miss Greedy.

And then she chuckled.

"I have a confession to make," she said.

"This isn't the only cake I baked today!
The first one looked so delicious,
I ate it for breakfast!"

She chuckled again.

"And the second one looked so delicious," she went on,
"I ate that one for my lunch!"

Mr Greedy grinned from ear to ear.

"Time for tea, Little Miss Greedy" he said.